The Secret Garden

igloobooks

Mary Lennox was nine years old when her parents died suddenly of cholera. She was sent away from her home in India to live in England with her uncle, Archibald Craven.

He wasn't there to greet her. Instead, Mary was met by Mrs Medlock, who was the housekeeper at Mr Craven's home. She took Mary north to Yorkshire, where Misselthwaite Manor stood on the edge of a wild and untamed moor. Everyone thought she was the most disagreeable-looking girl they had ever seen. It was true, for Mary was a sickly child who had been spoiled all her life by her servants in India. She had thin hair, a thin body and a sour expression.

On her first morning in her new home, Mary woke to the sound of Martha, the housemaid, cleaning the grate. She thought Martha would wash and dress her, but Martha refused. **"Children turn out fools, bein' washed an' dressed an' took out to walk like puppies!"** she said. Mary felt so far away from everything she knew that she began to cry.

Martha cheered her up with stories of her brother Dickon, and then she told Mary all about Misselthwaite Manor. **"One of the gardens is locked,"** said Martha. **"Mr Craven shut it up and buried the key when his wife died ten years ago."** Mary felt a flicker of interest at the mention of a locked garden. She decided she would go and look for it.

Mary wandered through the wintry gardens
until she came to a high, ivy-covered wall,
where a little robin chirruped a friendly greeting.
"Maybe this is the locked garden," thought Mary,
"but where is the door?" When she asked the
grumpy gardener, he warned her not to meddle.

After that, Mary spent every day outside. Then one morning, it was raining so heavily, she had to stay in. She was busy exploring the corridors of the manor when Mary thought she heard someone crying.

She asked Mrs Medlock about it, but the woman said sharply, **"You never heard any such thing!"** But Mary was sure she had.

The next day it stopped raining, so Mary dashed outside. By the hidden garden, she saw the little robin, hopping about and pecking in the soil. Looking down, she noticed something like a rusty ring of brass or iron. But it was more than a ring. It was a key!

The robin twittered excitedly and a sudden gust of wind blew at the loose curtain of ivy that grew over the wall. There was something behind it and, pushing the ivy aside, Mary saw that it was a door! She slotted in the key and turned it. Mary pushed the door and it creaked open.

At last, she stepped into the secret garden. Inside was the sweetest, most mysterious place anyone could imagine. There were climbing rose stems that grew in tangled trails over the trees and high walls. There were no petals or buds on anything, but it seemed to Mary like being shut out of the world in some fairy place.

Looking at the bare rose bushes, she wondered sadly if the garden was dead. Then, by a shady alcove, she noticed tiny shoots poking up among the yellow grass. **"The garden isn't dead!"** she cried and began pulling up the little weeds. Mary worked until it was time to go inside.

Mary had such red cheeks and bright eyes, and ate such a dinner that Martha was delighted. Mary asked her what might grow in a garden in spring, so she told her all about different types of flowers.

"I wish I had a little spade," said Mary. Martha said she could write to Dickon and he would fetch a tool set from the village.

Some days later, Mary met a boy of about twelve in the garden. **"I'm Dickon,"** he said. **"I've got th' garden tools."** He promised to keep Mary's work in the garden a secret.

Dickon showed Mary how to weed, and they spent hours clearing around the patches of shoots in the wild garden.

A few days later, Mary's uncle, Archibald Craven, finally returned to the manor. **"I am going away for the summer,"** he said. **"Is there anything that will make you happy while I'm gone?"** Mary asked for a piece of earth to grow seeds in, and Mr Craven agreed that she could choose any part of the garden she wished.

That night Mary heard crying again, and followed the sound upstairs. There, she found a boy, who said that he was her cousin Colin, Mr Craven's son. Colin explained that he never went out because he was always ill. Mary thought he was a strange, spoiled boy, but as it rained for a week after their first meeting, she visited him every day. She told him about the secret garden and he demanded to see it.

At last, the rain stopped and the sun shone. Mary raced outside and found Dickon digging in the garden. He had a tame fox called Captain and a crow called Soot. Mary was overjoyed to see her friend and as they worked in the garden that morning, she had never felt such happiness.

But late that night, Mary heard terrible screaming. Racing up to Colin's room, she found him wailing and crying. He was very angry at her for not coming to visit and insisted he would never get well. **"Stop that!"** yelled Mary. **"You are not ill. You just need fresh air and exercise!"**

Mary was the only person who had ever told Colin Craven what to do. Instead of being angry, he listened to her and the next day, Dickon came to take him outside.

Colin breathed the gusts of sweet, fresh air, and as they went into the secret garden...

... the first sight of it made him gasp in delight.

Everywhere, a green covering of tender little leaves had crept. Trees were laden with pink and white blossom, and all around were splashes of purple, gold and white.

Colin stared in wonder. "I **shall** get well," he cried. "And I shall live forever and ever!"

Mary and Dickon showed Colin around the garden. It was like being in the kingdom of a magic king and queen. Every moment was full of new things and every hour the sunshine grew more golden.

Then suddenly, the gardener's face appeared above the wall.

He was cross to see the children, saying Colin was too weak to be outside. Colin was so angry that he stood right up and Mary was sure the garden had worked its magic. As time went on, the secret garden bloomed and Colin grew stronger. Then, one day, Mr Craven returned to Misselthwaite Manor and to the garden he had locked ten years before.

He was amazed to see Colin so well. **"It was the garden that did it,"** cried Colin. **"And Mary and Dickon and the creatures and the magic."**

Colin told his father the story of how the garden had come alive and how it would never need to be a secret ever again.